Karen's Pilgrim

**Other books by
Ann M. Martin**

Leo the Magnificat
Rachel Parker, Kindergarten Show-off
Eleven Kids, One Summer
Ma and Pa Dracula
Yours Turly, Shirley
Ten Kids, No Pets
With You and Without You
Me and Katie (the Pest)
Stage Fright
Inside Out
Bummer Summer

For older readers:

Missing Since Monday
Just a Summer Romance
Slam Book

THE BABY-SITTERS CLUB series
THE BABY-SITTERS CLUB mysteries
THE KIDS IN MS. COLMAN'S CLASS series
BABY-SITTERS LITTLE SISTER series
(see inside book covers for a complete listing)

Little Sister

Karen's Pilgrim
Ann M. Martin

Illustrations by Susan Tang

A
LITTLE APPLE
PAPERBACK

SCHOLASTIC INC.
New York Toronto London Auckland Sydney

ISBN 0-590-06589-0

12 11 10 9 8 7 6 5 4 3 2 1   7 8 9/9 0 1 2/0

Printed in the U.S.A.   40
First Scholastic printing, November 1997

The author gratefully acknowledges
Stephanie Calmenson
for her help
with this book.

The author would like to thank
Carolyn Travers and the Plimoth Plantation staff
for their help in making sure
the facts in this story are correct.

Karen's Pilgrim

Thanks to Thanksgiving

"**W**ho would like to take attendance this morning?" asked my teacher, Ms. Colman.

My hand shot up so fast, I almost fell off my chair.

"All right, Karen. You have not had a turn in awhile," said Ms. Colman.

Yes! I like doing important jobs. Especially in Ms. Colman's second-grade class. Ms. Colman is a gigundoly wonderful teacher. She never raises her voice or gets angry at me. Even when I call out in class, she just asks me please to use my indoor voice.

Ms. Colman handed me the attendance book and a blue pencil. I started checking off names.

First I checked off my own name, Karen Brewer.

Then I checked off my two best friends, Nancy Dawes and Hannie Papadakis. They waved to me from the back of the room.

I used to sit at the back of the room with them. Then I got glasses and Ms. Colman moved me up front where I could see better. Actually, I have two pairs of glasses. I wear the blue pair for reading. I wear the pink pair the rest of the time. I happen to look excellent in both pink and blue. In case you are wondering, I have blonde hair and blue eyes. I also have a bunch of freckles. (They are light brown.)

After I checked off my best friends, I checked off my best enemy. Her name is Pamela Harding. She is a meanie-mo some-

times. Her two best friends are Jannie Gilbert and Leslie Morris. I checked off their names too.

Next I checked off Addie Sydney, who was peeling witch stickers off her wheelchair tray. She had a package of turkey stickers that she wanted to put on. That is because it was the beginning of November. Thanksgiving was on the way.

Natalie Springer popped up from under her desk. She had probably been pulling up her socks. They are always drooping. I checked off her name.

I checked off Ricky Torres, my pretend husband. (We got married on the playground one day at recess.) Then I checked off Ricky's friend Bobby Gianelli.

Terri and Tammy Barkan, who are twins, were in class. I checked off their names.

And I checked off a few more names. Then I handed the book and pencil back to Ms. Colman.

"Everyone is here," I said.

"Thank you, Karen," she replied. "All

right, class, I would like to tell you about a special assignment."

I sat up tall to listen. I love anything with the word *special* in it.

"As you know, Thanksgiving comes at the end of this month. There is a lot to learn about this wonderful holiday. I would like each of you to write a report about Thanksgiving. But that is not all. I would like you to make a presentation, as well. That will be the best way to share what we learn."

All right! Thanks to Thanksgiving, November was going to be an exciting month. I would get to stand in front of my class and make an important presentation. And this weekend I was going on a trip. I was going with my little-house family to visit Plymouth, Massachusetts. That is where Thanksgiving started.

But wait — you do not know about my two families. I have a little-house family and a big-house family.

Get ready. I have a lot to tell you.

2

My Two-Family Story

When I was little, I had just one family. I lived in a big house in Stoneybrook, Connecticut, with Mommy, Daddy, and Andrew. (Andrew is my little brother. He is four going on five.) I liked my family, but Mommy and Daddy fought a lot. That made everyone unhappy. Mommy and Daddy tried their best to get along. But it just did not work. So they told Andrew and me that they love us very much, but they could not live with each other anymore. Then they got a divorce.

Mommy moved with Andrew and me to a little house not too far away. She met a nice man named Seth and married him. Now Seth is my stepfather. Mommy, Seth, Andrew, and I live at the little house together. We have pets at the little house. They are Midgie, Seth's dog; Rocky, Seth's cat; Emily Junior, my pet rat; and Bob, Andrew's hermit crab.

Daddy stayed at the big house after the divorce. (It is the house he grew up in.) He met a nice woman named Elizabeth. Daddy and Elizabeth got married. So Elizabeth is my stepmother. Elizabeth was married once before and has four children. They are Kristy, who is thirteen and the best stepsister ever; David Michael, who is seven; and Sam and Charlie, who are so old they are in high school.

My other sister is Emily Michelle. She is two and a half. Daddy and Elizabeth adopted Emily from a faraway country called Vietnam. (I named my pet rat after her because I love her so much.)

After Emily came to live with us, Nannie moved in. Nannie is Elizabeth's mother. That makes her my stepgrandmother.

Those are all the people at the big house. These are the pets: Shannon, David Michael's big Bernese mountain dog puppy; Boo-Boo, Daddy's cranky old cat; Crystal Light the Second, my goldfish; and Goldfishie, Andrew's turkey. (Gotcha!) Emily Junior and Bob live at the big house whenever Andrew and I are there — which is every other month.

I have special names for my brother and me. I call us Andrew Two-Two and Karen Two-Two. (I thought up those names after Ms. Colman read a book to our class. It was called *Jacob Two-Two Meets the Hooded Fang*.) I gave us those names because we have two of so many things. We have two families and two sets of pets. We have two sets of toys and clothes and books — one set at each house. That makes going back and forth between our houses easier. I have two bicycles, one at each house, and so does Andrew. (I helped him learn to ride a two-wheeler.) I have two stuffed cats. (Goosie lives at the little house. Moosie lives at the big house.) And you already know that I have two best friends. Nancy lives next door to the little house. Hannie lives across the street and one house down from the big house.

Like I said, Andrew and I switch houses every month. Where were we in November? At the little house. And my little-house family was going on a trip. I could hardly wait.

3

Are We There Yet?

I counted the days until my trip. Tuesday. Wednesday. Thursday. Friday — trip day!

School went by in a blur. All I could think about was going to the place where real Pilgrims once lived.

After school I did not ride the school bus home. Mommy, Seth, and Andrew were waiting to pick me up.

"See you Monday!" I called to my friends.

"Have a great time," said Hannie.

"Tell us everything when you get back," said Nancy.

Pamela was standing near us.

"Where are you going?" she asked.

"I am going to Plymouth, Massachusetts. To a place where the real Pilgrims lived," I said.

"Oh, you mean Plimoth Plantation. I have been there twice already," said Pamela.

Boo. Pamela always has to be first and best.

"Well, I am glad it is my first time. First times are the most fun," I said.

I heard Mommy calling me. I waved good-bye to my friends and ran to the car. I was glad to be going someplace new. And I was glad to be getting away from Pamela Harding.

"How was school?" said Mommy.

"It was okay," I replied.

"Would you like a snack?" asked Seth as we drove off.

"Sure," I replied. I am always hungry after school.

"Me too," said Andrew.

We had crackers with peanut butter, and apple juice. While we were eating, Mommy read to us from a Plimoth Plantation brochure.

"Listen to the names of some of the foods the Pilgrims ate," said Mommy. "Seethed lobster. Savory pudding of hominy. Crimped fish. Colewart sallet. Cheate bread."

"Ooh, it is bad to cheat," said Andrew with his mouth full of crackers. "That bread is going to get in trouble."

Seth laughed. "I wonder what cheate bread is."

"We can ask when we get there," said Mommy. "The brochure says the people we meet will be happy to answer our questions."

I finished my snack.

"I have to go to the bathroom," I said.

"Me too," said Andrew.

Seth pulled off the highway at the first rest stop, even though we had just gotten *on* the highway. We used the bathrooms, then found the highway again.

"I am bored," I said after we had driven a little way.

"Me too," said Andrew, kicking his seat.

Mommy and Seth played a game of Twenty Questions with us. Then we sang songs. We stopped for supper. Then we got back on the road.

"Are we there yet?" I asked.

"Not yet," replied Seth.

We played more games. We sang more songs.

"Are we there yet?" I asked.

"Almost," replied Seth.

He pulled off the highway and onto smaller roads. Finally we stopped at the water. It was dark outside, but we could see a tall ship.

"Are we there yet?" asked Andrew.

"We sure are," said Seth. "That is the *Mayflower Two*. It was made to look like the boat the Pilgrims sailed."

"Wow!" said Andrew. He loves boats.

"The Pilgrims' trip from England to

America took a lot longer than our trip from Stoneybrook," said Mommy.

"And they did not have a comfortable hotel to stay in. But we do," said Seth.

I love hotels. We drove to ours and settled in. In the bathroom were little soaps wrapped in paper. Fresh sheets were on the beds. I fell asleep as soon as my head hit the pillow.

4

Welcome to Plimoth Plantation

We woke up early on Saturday morning. We ate breakfast in the hotel coffee shop, then drove to Plimoth Plantation.

Seth bought four tickets good for two days of visiting. I wanted to go straight to the village. But Mommy and Seth wanted to see the orientation show.

"I would rather see real things," I said.

"The show is short," Mommy replied. "Seeing it will help you understand the village better."

We found four seats in the screening

room. The program started right away. Pictures flashed on the screen. The narrator said Plimoth Plantation was a re-creation of the real village from the year 1627.

I was surprised that the village looked so cheerful and colorful. I thought Pilgrims wore black clothes and tall black hats all the time.

The voice said the people we would meet in the village are called role players. It is their job to talk and act the way the Pilgrims did in 1627. I wondered how they knew what life was like all the way back then. The voice must have read my mind, because it answered my question right away.

"We learned about this historical village through painstaking research. We continue to learn new things as more objects from the past are uncovered," said the voice.

We were told we could ask the role players as many questions as we liked. I already had a long list.

I clapped when the show ended. It was very good. And short.

"I have an idea," said Seth. "How about

starting at the *Mayflower Two*? That way we will see the sights in the same order the Pilgrims did."

This sounded like a good idea to me. And Andrew could not wait to get back to the boat he had seen the night before.

We got in the car and drove to the water. The *Mayflower Two* looked even prettier in the daylight.

"Ahoy!" said Andrew. He waved a make-believe sword.

"There were no pirates on this boat. They were Pilgrims," I said.

We stepped on board and back into history. We saw men swabbing decks and fixing masts. Two women sat together. One was knitting; the other was reading aloud from a Bible.

We walked down to the cabins. A mother was on a bed with her daughter.

"Mother, I am feeling very poorly," said the girl.

"Father will be here soon with medicine for thee," the mother replied.

"Maybe she needs to go to a doctor," I whispered.

"There were one hundred and three people crowded together on this ship," said Seth. "Many of them got sick, and there was only one doctor to help them as they crossed the sea. It was a difficult trip."

"The trip from England to where they finally settled in Plymouth took over two months," said Mommy.

"What did the children do if they did not go to school?" I asked.

"It was very hard for them," said Mommy. "There was no room to run and play. They had little fresh food to eat. They had to wear the same clothes every day. And most of them had to sleep on beds on the ship's hard, cold floor."

"I want to go home!" cried Andrew.

Mommy put her arms around him. "I am sorry I scared you," she said. "You do not have to worry. You have warm clothes, good food, and two houses to live in."

Andrew was still crying. "I want to go home!"

Mommy took Andrew off the boat. Seth and I stayed and walked around some more. I even got to help tie a rope to the ship. I felt like a true Pilgrim.

A Walk Around
the Village

When Seth and I had seen everything we wanted to see, we left the boat. We found Andrew and Mommy looking in the windows of a bakery.

"Karen! This is where they make cheater's bread!" Andrew said.

"Cheate bread," said Mommy. "Should we try some?"

"Yes, please!" Andrew and I said together.

Cheate bread is a lot like regular bread. Only it is made into little rolls. It is delicious.

After our snack, we drove back to the village. I felt as though I had been there before. That is because it looked just the way it did in the orientation show.

The people were wearing colorful clothing. They were laughing and talking, working and playing. Even though I knew they were just pretending to be Pilgrims, and even though lots of other people were visiting Plimoth Plantation that day, just the way my family and I were, I forgot about real life as I walked through the village. I felt as if I had walked back in time to 1627, when the Pilgrims lived.

"Good day to you. And how do you fare?" asked a man passing by.

He seemed friendly, even though he was carrying a big saw over his shoulder.

"I fare fine, thank you. How are you?" I replied.

"Very well. I am on my way to saw timbers, with which to build a house for my family," replied the man. "Come join me if it please you."

"Thank you!" said Seth.

I was not surprised that Seth was excited. He is a carpenter. But sawing wood did not sound so exciting to me. I was more interested in two girls playing nearby.

"I want to go over there," I said.

"I want to saw wood," said Andrew.

"No problem," said Seth. "We can split up and meet in a couple of hours at the Visitors' Center."

Mommy walked and I ran to where the girls were playing.

"I know that game! It is Fox and Geese," I said.

"It is our favorite," replied one of the girls.

"You played this game all the way back in the sixteen hundreds?" I asked.

"We play it, yes," replied the girl. "You can play the next round if you like."

"When you finish the round, it will be time for us to return home," said a woman standing near us.

"Yes, Mother," said the girl. She turned to

me and said, "You are welcome to come along."

"Cool!" I cried. I was going to a Pilgrim girl's house!

"By the way, my name is Remember," said the girl. "I am twelve."

"I am Karen Brewer. I am seven. And this is my mom," I replied.

When the game of Fox and Geese was over, Mommy and I followed Remember and her mother home.

6

Lots of Questions

On the way, I studied Remember's clothes. They did not look anything like mine. I was wearing purple leggings, pink sneakers, a gray sweatshirt, and a navy blue jacket. Remember was wearing a white bonnet, brown jacket, white apron, long cranberry skirt, and tan coat. Her skirt looked a lot bigger than she did.

"Do you have a lot of stuff on under there? You look very puffy," I said.

As soon as I asked my question, I felt a little bit sorry. I hoped I had not hurt Remem-

25

ber's feelings. I could tell by her answer that I had not.

"Aye, I do wear a number of garments. It takes me a long time to dress every day. Next to my skin I wear a linen shift. Then I put on stockings and garters to hold them up. Over these garments, I put on three petticoats. This one of sad red is the topmost," said Remember.

"Wow, that sure is a lot," I replied.

"There is more," said Remember. "I put on my apron and coif and — "

"What is a coif?" I asked.

"It is the linen cap on my head. Then I put on my shoes and my waistcoat. My waistcoat has many buttons and I must be sure to button every one," said Remember.

I knew her waistcoat was her jacket. I counted the buttons on it. There were fifteen!

"If I had to do all that dressing, I would be late for school," I said.

"No. You would get up early the way I

do," said Remember. "And you would not dillydally in the morning."

"Here we are," said Remember's mother. "Welcome to our home."

Remember's clothes did not look like my clothes. And her house did not look like either of my two houses. Her house was all gray wood. Inside was a dirt floor. Still, it felt nice and cozy. It smelled very good too.

"What smells so delicious?" asked Mommy.

"We are cooking duck with fruit and spices," said Remember's mother. "It has been cooking since early morning."

"Will we make the corn bread now?" asked Remember.

"Yes," replied her mother. "Perhaps Karen will help us."

"Sure," I said. "Just tell me what to do."

It was my job to measure. I measured the water that went into a pot. I poured in the cornmeal. Remember and I took turns stirring. Remember said that when the batter was ready, the bread would bake in the oven. The oven was outside.

While we stirred, I asked Remember more questions. I asked about cheate bread.

"It is a funny name for bread," I said.

Remember said no one knew why it was called that. It just was.

"The orientation show said you had to leave your home in England and sail all the way here to be free. Do you miss your home a lot?" I asked.

"Yes, I miss my friends. And the voyage was very difficult. I was sick most of the time. It took many months for me to get well," said Remember. "But my life here is good. I have made new friends and my parents are happy."

"We needed to come here to be free to worship the way God shows us. It was worth the long trip and many hardships," said Remember's mother.

I asked more questions and listened carefully to every answer. I needed the informa-

tion for my school report. But even if I were not working on a report, I would still have wanted to know all I could about this Pilgrim girl named Remember. I wanted to know just because I liked her.

7

Snap!

"Shall we take Karen and her mother for a walk before Father comes home for the evening meal?" asked Remember's mother.

"Did you say evening? We have not even had lunch yet!" I said.

Mommy looked at her watch and gasped. "Karen, we better go meet Seth and Andrew. We can come back later."

We excused ourselves and ran to the Visitors' Center where Seth and Andrew were waiting. The four of us ate a quick, late lunch at the Visitors' Center. We had not eaten since our cheate-bread snack, so we were hungry.

"How do you like Plimoth Plantation?" Seth asked.

"I am having a great time," I said. "I made a new friend named Remember."

"I helped saw wood. Then I went to where a real Indian lived," said Andrew.

"The Indians who lived near the village were a great help to the Pilgrims," said Seth. "One Indian named Squanto even lived with the Pilgrims. He taught them all about farming and hunting."

This sounded important for my school report. I would have to ask Seth about the Indians later.

"Who wants to see some more of the village?" asked Mommy.

"Me!" said Andrew and I together.

Seth and Andrew headed toward a group of men gathered around the entrance to one of the buildings.

Mommy and I walked around. I saw lots of other families who were visiting. But I saw lots of Pilgrim role players too. When I watched them, I forgot about the visitors.

I wondered what Remember was doing. "Can we go back to see Remember and her mother?" I asked.

"Okay. Let's see if we can find their house," Mommy replied.

When we found the house, Remember was just coming out the door. She was carrying a wooden bucket.

"Remember!" I called. "Hi! It's me. I mean, it is I, Karen! What are you doing?"

"I am going to milk our goat. You may come and watch, if it please you," Remember answered.

"Truly!" I replied.

Remember's mother had used that word a few times. I tried to say it just the way she had. I was practicing to be a role player. It would be fun to be a role player with Remember. I would have to ask her about that.

Remember was already at the goat pen. The goat was so cute. She was brown and tan with a white spot on her side.

"What is her name?" I asked.

"We call her Fillpail," said Remember. 'Come, I will show you how I milk her."

Fillpail was cute. But she was crabby. The first time Remember tried to milk her, she kicked. Remember jumped out of the way just in time. Finally Fillpail calmed down. The milk squirted loudly into Remember's wooden bucket.

Just as Remember was finishing, I heard a grunting sound in the next pen. A big, dark, hairy animal poked its snout through the fence.

"What kind of animal is that? It sounds like a pig. And it has a pig's snout. But it does not look like any pig I have ever seen," I said.

"It is the only kind of pig we know," said Remember.

Just then I thought of something important. I had forgotten to take pictures! I took my camera out of my knapsack and started snapping.

"I need pictures for my school report," I explained to Remember.

I took pictures of Remember milking Fill-pail. I tried to take pictures of the pig. But he was not very cooperative. As soon as I came near him, he turned and trotted away.

Remember found some scraps and held them out to the pig. He came running. *Snap. Snap.* I got two excellent shots.

"Can I get pictures of your house now?" I asked when we were inside again.

"Of course," replied Remember's mother. "After that, you may help us lay the table, if you would be so kind."

I took some more pictures, then helped Remember and her mother set the table. They used wooden plates and bowls and spoons. Their drinking cups were made of clay or metal.

"Where are the forks?" I asked.

"We do not have forks. We use knives, spoons, and our hands to eat," said Remember.

"I like to eat with my hands," I said.

When the table was set, I noticed that some other families were at the door, looking in. I also noticed that it was getting dark outside.

"It is time for us to go, Karen," said Mommy.

I wished I could spend more time with Remember. I really liked her.

"Thank you for helping me, Karen," she said.

"Come see us again," said Remember's mother.

Mommy and I said good-bye and headed for the Visitors' Center. When we got there, Andrew was in the middle of a big yawn. We had all had a busy day.

8

Souvenirs

We were up early again on Sunday. After breakfast Seth drove us to the water to see Plymouth Rock.

"I would not want to miss seeing that," he said.

It looked like an ordinary rock to me. Only it was big and had the number 1620 carved in it.

"It is believed that this rock is near the very spot where the Pilgrims set foot in Plymouth," said Mommy.

Suddenly the rock did not look so ordinary. Now it looked special. I closed my eyes and made believe I was a Pilgrim girl stepping on the land for the first time. I made believe I was Remember.

"Can we go back to the village?" I asked when I opened my eyes again. "Perchance I will see Remember."

"Per-what?" asked Andrew.

"Perchance. That is the Pilgrim word for maybe," I replied. (It is another word Remember's mother had used.)

"We can take a quick walk around the village. Then we should go to the crafts center," said Seth. "Things there are made just the way they were made in the seventeenth century. Next door is a shop where we can buy souvenirs."

As soon as I heard *souvenirs*, I said, "Let's go!"

At the village some people were singing a hymn. We stood and listened. Then I headed for Remember's house. She was inside stirring something that smelled very good.

"Good day!" said Remember's mother.

"How fare thee, Karen?" asked Remember.

"I fare very well," I replied. "What are you cooking?"

"I am helping to make Indian corn pudding. It is Indian corn cooked with spices, fruit, and milk," said Remember.

It smelled delicious. Andrew and I wanted to taste it. But Mommy and Seth said it was time to go. Once again I had to say good-bye to Remember. This time I did not expect to see her again.

I was feeling sad on the way to the crafts house. But once we got there, I did not have time to be sad. There was so much going on.

A woman was weaving cloth. A man was making a table. Someone else was making a pitcher out of clay.

We watched everything and talked to the people working. Then we headed for the museum shop.

I wanted to buy souvenirs for three people: Hannie, Nancy, and me. I saw my own present right away.

"Mommy, look at that poppet doll. May I get it, please?" I said.

It looked just like the doll I had seen on Remember's bed. It was made of white cloth with a face embroidered on it. The doll was wearing a brown dress and a white apron.

"Mommy, please!" I said.

I held out the doll. Mommy looked at the price.

"It is very expensive, Karen. I do not think you can afford to buy it," said Mommy.

I looked at the price. It *was* expensive. Even if I spent all of my money and did not buy anything for Hannie and Nancy, I still would not have enough.

I gave the doll a hug and put it back on the shelf. I looked at the other souvenirs. I saw some very good ones. I found a bag of clay marbles, a quill pen with a beautiful feather, and an ink packet to go with the pen. I thought these would be good souvenirs for my presentation. I bought them for myself. Then I bought two more bags of marbles, one for Hannie and one for Nancy. I had a little money left over, so I bought three postcards, one each for Hannie and Nancy and me.

I also picked up some free Plimoth Plantation brochures. They had color pictures and lots of information. I thought they would be very helpful for my school report.

"It is time to head back to Stoneybrook," said Seth. "We do not want to get back too late."

The ride home went fast. That is because I slept most of the way. And I had a wonderful dream. I dreamed I was a Pilgrim child. Remember was my big sister. The year was 1627.

No Fair!

When I woke up on Monday morning, I was no longer in Plymouth in 1627. I had returned to my real life in Stoneybrook, Connecticut. It was time to get ready for school.

I wrapped the two bags of marbles in bright-colored tissue paper. I taped a Plimoth Plantation postcard on each one. I was sure these gifts would make Hannie and Nancy gigundoly happy.

When Nancy and I reached school, Hannie was already there. I gave my friends their gifts.

"These marbles are cool, Karen. Thank you," said Nancy.

"I've never seen clay marbles before," said Hannie. "And the postcard is really pretty too. Thanks."

"I wish you could have come on my trip," I said. "It was so much fun. I made friends with a twelve-year-old Pilgrim girl. And look what I got for my presentation."

I pulled out the quill pen and the ink packet.

"This is the kind of pen the Pilgrims used," I said.

Suddenly Pamela was standing next to me.

"I got the same pen and three different colored ink packets," she said. "I brought them to show Ms. Colman today. And look what else I have."

She pulled the pen and three ink packets out of her school bag. Then she pulled out a bag of marbles. And *then* she pulled one more thing out of her bag. A poppet doll.

"Isn't she cute?" said Pamela. "Did you get one too?"

"I was going to," I said. "But the girl in front of me bought the last one."

I do not like to lie. But I did not want to tell Pamela the doll was too expensive for me. I would tell my friends the truth later.

"Too bad for you," said Pamela.

Just then Ms. Colman came into the room. Pamela was about to show her the souvenirs when I stopped her.

"Pamela, I know you are going to show those things to Ms. Colman. But you are not going to use them all in your presentation, right?" I said.

"Wrong," Pamela replied. "I want to show all my Plimoth Plantation souvenirs."

"Could you please not show the marbles or the pen-and-ink set? Those are the things I am going to present," I said.

"Too bad again," said Pamela. "Why should I not show them when I have them?"

"Because you have the poppet doll. That is special enough," I replied.

"But my presentation will be more special with *all* my souvenirs," said Pamela. She

turned and walked to Ms. Colman's desk.

I was so mad. If Pamela showed all her souvenirs, then I would have nothing special to show. And Pamela's presentation was going to be on Monday. Mine would not be until Tuesday. Who would want to see the same things twice?

It was no fair!

10

Meanie-mo

At recess I told my friends the truth about the poppet doll.

"I could not spend that much money on a souvenir either," said Nancy.

"Me neither," said Hannie. "Maybe Pamela will change her mind about the souvenirs. Maybe if you ask really nicely."

I decided to try. Again. I ran across the playground to the swings. That is where Pamela, Jannie, and Leslie were playing.

"Hi," I said. "Did Ms. Colman like your souvenirs?"

47

"She loved them," replied Pamela.

"I bet she liked the poppet doll the best," I said.

I thought if that were true, Pamela might leave the other souvenirs at home.

"She liked them *all*," said Pamela. "That is why I am bringing them *all* to my presentation."

"It would be really nice of you to leave the other things at home," I said.

"No way," said Pamela.

"Please?"

"No."

I walked away. I was going to give a report to Hannie and Nancy.

"What did she say?" asked Hannie.

"She said 'No way' and 'No'."

"She is being a meanie-mo," said Nancy.

"You can try again later," said Hannie.

After recess we went to our school library. I had seen a book about the Pilgrims that I needed for my report. I looked on the shelves, but it was not there anymore. And I knew it was not at the public library.

"Is there something I can help you with?" asked Mr. Counts, our librarian.

"I would like to borrow *The Pilgrims' First Thanksgiving*. But I cannot find it," I said.

"Let me check my records." Mr. Counts looked at his computer screen. "Yes, that book is out. In fact, a girl in your class borrowed it. Maybe she will let you look at it."

"Who borrowed it?" I asked.

"Pamela Harding," replied Mr. Counts.

Boo. I did not think a meanie-mo like Pamela would let me look at her library book. But I decided to ask her anyway.

I found her at a table reading a book about Squanto, the Indian who had helped the Pilgrims.

"Excuse me, Pamela," I said. I was trying very hard to be polite.

"Forget it, Karen. I am bringing the souvenirs and that is final," Pamela said before I had a chance to ask my question.

"That is not what I was going to ask," I said. "But now that you mention it, why can't you leave them at home? It would not hurt you to be nice, you know."

"I am just doing my presentation," said Pamela.

"Well, you are being mean. And it is not the Pilgrim spirit to be mean!" I said.

"Shh. Quiet in the library, please," said Mr. Counts.

"Anyway, I was not going to ask about the souvenirs. I want to ask if I could look at the Thanksgiving book you borrowed. It is the only copy," I said.

"Since you think I am such a meanie, the answer to your question is no," said Pamela. "It just so happens it is due back tomorrow. But I think I will check it out again. I may have missed a few facts."

"Pamela," I said, stamping my foot. "You are the biggest meanie-mo ever!"

"Sticks and stones may break my bones. But I'm the one with the book and souvenirs. So there," said Pamela.

I stomped over to my friends to give them the latest meanie-mo report.

11

Karen's Report

I tried talking to Pamela again on Tuesday. But she would not change her mind.

"It just is not fair," I said to Mommy. I was eating my after-school snack. (Andrew was at a friend's house.)

"There is nothing more you can do about Pamela," said Mommy. "You will have to think about your report in a new way. Maybe the souvenirs should not be such an important part of your presentation anymore."

"But I want to do something exciting," I said. "Something the class will remember."

The word *remember* made me think of my Pilgrim friend. I could still show my pictures of her. And I could show pictures of all of Plimoth Plantation, from the brochures we had brought home.

I found the brochures on my desk. All of a sudden I saw something I had not noticed before — information about a special program. It said the role players sometimes visited schools.

"Maybe Remember could visit our class for my presentation," I said. I showed Mommy the brochure. "That would be so exciting!"

"Your report is only a week away, Karen," said Mommy. "I am sure the role players are all booked up."

"But we can try. Maybe no one else wanted a role player that day," I said. "Can't we just call and ask?"

"I don't know," said Mommy. "I do not want you to get your hopes up and then be disappointed."

"I will be more disappointed if we do not even try," I said.

So Mommy dialed the phone number on the Plimoth Plantation brochure.

"Hello, I would like to speak with someone about making a school visit," said Mommy. "Yes, thank you. I will hold."

I was so excited that I started to jump up and down.

"Please say yes. Please, please, please!" I said.

"Would it be possible to arrange for a school visit next Tuesday?" I heard Mommy ask. She listened for a moment, then said, "Yes, I see. You are already booked. May I leave my name and number in case there is a cancellation?"

I was not jumping up and down anymore. Mommy was right. I was disappointed. But I was still glad we had tried.

"I am sorry," said Mommy when she hung up the phone. "But I think you should work on your report now. I am sure you will find a way to make it interesting even without a special visitor."

I went upstairs and took out my notebook. I knew a lot of interesting facts about Thanksgiving. I decided to start writing about the first Thanksgiving celebration in Plymouth.

IN 1621, THE PILGRIMS HAD A VERY GOOD HARVEST. THEY WANTED TO GIVE THANKS FOR IT. SO THEY HAD A FESTIVAL THAT LASTED FOR THREE DAYS. THE MEN HUNTED. THE WOMEN COOKED. ABOUT NINETY INDIANS CAME WITH FIVE DEER FOR THE FEAST. THERE WAS PLENTY OF MEAT, FISH, AND CORN BREAD FOR EVERYONE TO EAT.

I looked at what I had written. I checked my spelling. There were no mistakes. (I am a very good speller.) Then I continued the story.

THERE WERE MANY OTHER THANKSGIVING CELEBRATIONS. WHENEVER SOMETHING EXTRA GOOD HAPPENED — ESPECIALLY A GOOD HARVEST OR A NEEDED RAINFALL — AN IMPORTANT PERSON IN A TOWN WOULD CALL FOR A DAY OF THANKS.

THEN IN THE 1800s A FAMOUS WRITER NAMED

SARA JOSEPHA HALE WORKED HARD TO TURN THANKS-
GIVING INTO A NATIONAL HOLIDAY. FINALLY, IN 1863,
PRESIDENT ABRAHAM LINCOLN DECLARED THE LAST
THURSDAY IN NOVEMBER A GENERAL DAY OF THANKS-
GIVING. THAT DAY BECAME OUR THANKSGIVING
HOLIDAY IN AMERICA UNTIL 1941. THEN PRESIDENT
FRANKLIN DELANO ROOSEVELT CHANGED THE HOLIDAY
TO THE FOURTH THURSDAY IN NOVEMBER. AND THAT IS
THE DAY WE CELEBRATE THANKSGIVING!

I read my report. It might not be as exciting as a poppet doll. But it was still pretty
good.

The Best Secret

At school the next day I did not say one word to Pamela Harding. I could tell she expected me to. But I did not do it. By the end of the day I would not even look in her direction.

When I got home after school, I waved good-bye to Nancy. We could not play because we were going to work on our reports and presentations.

The phone was ringing when I walked through our front door. Mommy answered it.

"Yes, this is Lisa Engle," she said. "Oh, really? That is wonderful news. My daughter just walked in. She will be thrilled."

"Can a Pilgrim come to visit?" I cried.

Mommy nodded.

"Ask them for Remember, Mommy!" I said.

Mommy nodded again. She was listening and writing things down.

"I did not realize it costs that much. But you say you can visit several classrooms in one day? That will be wonderful for the whole school," said Mommy.

She was smiling.

"Do not forget to ask about Remember," I whispered.

Mommy asked if Remember and her mother could come.

She listened for a bit, then said, "Oh, I see. Well, thank you for the information."

"What happened? What did they say?" I asked when she hung up.

"The people at Plimoth Plantation said that children are not allowed to make school

visits. The visits are made only by adult Pilgrims," replied Mommy.

Boo. I wanted Remember to come. But a visit from a grown-up Pilgrim would still be exciting.

"The visit will cost over two hundred dollars," said Mommy. "I will need to call the head of our parents' association right away. I am sure they can help pay for an event that is so special."

"I would like the visit to be a surprise to my class. Is that okay, Mommy?" I asked.

"You will have to ask Ms. Colman. It will be up to her to decide," replied Mommy.

We decided to call Ms. Colman at home. Mommy did not think my teacher would mind.

Guess what! Ms. Colman thought the visit was a wonderful idea. And she thought the surprise would be a lot of fun for my class.

I was so excited. This was going to be one of my best surprises ever!

13

Pamela's Presentation

When I arrived at school on Friday, Pamela was bragging to her friends about her presentation. I could tell she was talking louder than usual so that I would hear.

"This is going to be great. I have so many good things to show," she said.

"The meanie-mo strikes again," I whispered to Hannie and Nancy.

"We will see on Monday how great her presentation is," Hannie whispered back.

I was bursting to tell Pamela about my surprise. I wanted to tell my friends too. But for once my lips were sealed. I did not want to ruin my best secret ever.

Ms. Colman asked us to take our seats then.

On the way to her desk, Pamela said, "Hi, Karen. Is your presentation ready yet?"

"Almost. I will have everything I need on Tuesday," I replied. I gave her my best secret-surprise smile. I would have to write a new report. But I did not care. I was going to have a *Pilgrim* in my presentation!

I kept my secret all day on Friday. I did not even give in and tell my friends.

Over the weekend, I worked on my speech. I practiced reciting it to Goosie. I could tell he was impressed.

At school on Monday afternoon, the presentations began. Pamela's was the very first one. She read a speech she had written in her notebook. (I had already memorized mine.)

"My presentation is about my *two* trips to Plimoth Plantation," said Pamela. "This historical village is in the state of Massachusetts. People who are called role players talk and act just like Pilgrims in the sixteen hundreds."

Pamela told us a lot of interesting facts about the village. Then she showed us her souvenirs. Every single one of them.

"And that is the story of Plimoth Plantation," she said.

"Thank you, Pamela. That was a very good presentation," said Ms. Colman.

My classmates clapped. I clapped too. Only not very loudly. Pamela might think she had told the whole story of Plimoth Plantation. But I had more to tell and plenty more to show. I had a real, live, walking, talking souvenir.

14

Welcome to Stoneybrook

On Tuesday morning we heard Hannie's presentation, then Nancy's.

Hannie had written a story in rhyme about the Pilgrims coming to America on the *Mayflower*. She had made a diorama of a ship that moved across the ocean.

Nancy dressed up as Squanto the Indian and told about the first Thanksgiving feast. She brought Indian corn for everyone to taste.

My friends' presentations were excellent.

I was gigundoly proud of them. I liked my other classmates' presentations too.

But as the morning passed, I could not think of anything but my visitor. At lunchtime I could hardly even eat. All I could do was stare at the clock on the lunchroom wall. I was supposed to be at the principal's office at one o'clock to meet my Pilgrim visitor.

I wished Remember could be the visitor today. But I knew that was not possible. I wondered who my Pilgrim would be.

"Karen, are you all right? You hardly ate anything," said Hannie.

I looked down at my sandwich. Only two bites were gone.

"I am okay," I replied. "But I think I will stay inside at recess today."

I was not lying to my friends. It was true that I was staying inside. I just did not tell them why.

I waited until five minutes to one. Then I went to see Ms. Titus, the principal. When

I reached her office, I could hardly believe my eyes. She was talking to my visitors — Remember and her mother! Yippee!

"Your younger visitor is not here officially, Karen," Ms. Titus said to me. "She received special permission to travel here today."

I wanted to jump up and down and shout, "Yes!" But I was in the principal's office. So I tried my hardest to act grown-up.

"I am so happy to see you!" I said.

"We are happy to see thee again, Karen," said Remember. "And we are pleased to visit thy school."

Remember and her mother were dressed in their Pilgrim clothes and speaking the way the Pilgrims did. It seemed as though they had stepped out of the pages of a history book and arrived special delivery at Stoneybrook Academy.

"Are you ready to escort your visitors to your classroom?" asked Ms. Titus. "I understand that you have not said anything to the other students. Your visitors will be quite a surprise."

"They sure will be!" I said.

I linked arms with Remember and her mother and walked them through the halls to my classroom. My Thanksgiving presentation was about to begin.

15

Karen's Important Job

I opened the door to my classroom and led Remember and her mother inside.

I smiled at Ms. Colman and waved to Hannie and Nancy. I saw Pamela's eyes open wide and her mouth drop open. Ms. Two-Time Visitor With All the Souvenirs was definitely surprised. There was no way her cloth poppet doll could seem as special as my real live Pilgrims.

The kids in my class were all whispering to each other. I heard a few of them say, "Wow!" and "Cool!" I just loved standing at

the front of the room with my guests.

"All right, class, please settle down so we can welcome our visitors," said Ms. Colman. "Karen, will you introduce us?"

"These are my Pilgrim friends from Plimoth Plantation. They are here from the year sixteen twenty-seven to talk about their lives. They will tell you their story," I said.

Everyone clapped for my guests. Then Remember stepped forward.

"My name is Remember Allerton. I sailed onboard a ship called *Mayflower* from England to America in the year sixteen twenty. My family wanted to live where we could be free to pray the way God showed us."

Remember stepped back and her mother stepped forward.

"My name is Fear Allerton. I am Remember's mother. I am grateful that my family and I were strong enough to reach America. Our life in New England was a struggle at first. But with the help of our Indian neighbors, we learned to survive. We give thanks every day for our health and our freedom."

Remember came forward again. She stood by her mother and together they talked some more about everyday life in 1627. They showed the class wooden spoons, some candles, and a few other things they had brought with them.

When they finished, Remember's mother smiled and said, "We are happy to be visiting you today. We would be pleased to answer your questions."

A few hands went up right away.

"Karen, I will leave it to you to call on your classmates. This is *your* presentation," Ms. Colman said.

She sat down at her desk and let me take over. This was one of my most important jobs ever!

16

How Fare Thee?

I called on Hannie first.

"My presentation was about the *Mayflower*," she said. "Could you please tell me what the trip was really like?"

"It was a very difficult journey," replied Remember. "We were crowded together in the ship. And there were many storms. One storm damaged our ship so badly, we almost had to turn back. But we decided to continue."

"We set sail in September when it was warm," said Remember's mother. "We did not reach New England until November, when it was cold. But the trip was worth every hardship."

"Thank you," said Hannie.

I called on Ricky next.

"When you landed, where did you live?" he asked.

"Parties of men explored the coast until they found a place with freshwater and good soil for planting. We built our houses there. While our men were building, we had to continue living crowded together in the *Mayflower*," replied Remember's mother.

Nancy wanted to know where the children go to school.

"There are no schools in New Plymouth," replied Remember. "We children learn to read and write from our parents. Some of the men learned about hunting and growing Indian corn from Squanto. And our parents teach us to behave properly."

Bobby wanted to know what kinds of games the children like to play. I told him that they play Fox and Geese.

Then Terri asked about the clothes the Pilgrims wear.

"Our clothes are of good English wool and Dutch linen," said Remember's mother.

"We have brought some clothing for two of you to try on," said Remember.

This was so cool. In no time I was putting on petticoats, an apron, and a coif. Ricky was picked to wear the boy's clothes. He put on knee-length pants, called breeches, and a jacket.

We all tried talking the way the Pilgrims did.

"How farest thou?" Nancy asked me.

"Quite well, good friend," I replied.

"Wilst thou be coming to the Thanksgiving feast?" I asked Hannie.

"If it so pleases thee," Hannie replied.

"It pleaseth me very well," I said.

I turned to Remember and said, "Wilst thou come and be our guest of honor?"

"I thank thee," Remember replied.

After a little while I asked Ms. Colman to help me get everyone's attention. It was time for me to make my presentation.

I Am a Pilgrim Girl

As soon as the class was quiet, I began.

"I loved going to Plimoth Plantation," I said. "It was like walking through the pages of a history book. Thanks to Remember, I learned what it might have felt like to be a Pilgrim child. I thought you would like to know too, so I wrote this story."

I stopped to straighten my coif and smooth my petticoats. I cleared my throat. Then I continued.

"I am a Pilgrim girl," I said. "I came to America because in England we were not

free to pray the way we wanted. I left my house, my toys, and my friends behind. I missed them so much. The trip across the ocean was very hard. I tried not to cry or complain, but a few times I could not help it. Finally we reached America. It was a cold and strange place. But an Indian named Squanto taught us many things that helped us survive. We built our houses. We grew our food. We stayed and grew strong.

"I am a Pilgrim girl and that is my story. I hope when you celebrate Thanksgiving you will think of me and my family and how hard we worked to be free."

The next thing I knew, everyone in the room was clapping and cheering for me. My presentation was a big hit.

It was time for Remember and her mother to leave. Ricky and I returned our Pilgrim clothes.

"Thank you for coming," Ms. Colman said to our guests. "You have made this a very special day for us. Karen, would you like to walk your guests back to Ms. Titus's office?"

"Sure," I replied.

I led them through the halls very slowly. I did not want to say good-bye too soon.

When I reached Ms. Titus's office, there was another surprise. Mommy was there waiting for us.

"Hi, how did it go?" she asked.

"It was the best presentation ever!" I replied.

"I thought it might be nice for all of us to go out for ice cream after school. Could you be our guests?" Mommy asked Remember's mother.

"We have one more class to visit. After that we would be delighted," Remember's mother replied.

"Thank thee, Mommy!" I said.

My presentation was done, but the fun was not over yet.

Brianna Murphy

There were two more presentations in my class. They were both very good. Then it was time to go home.

When I got outside, I saw Mommy. But I did not see Remember and her mother. I was worried. Maybe they could not stay for ice cream after all. Maybe they had left without even saying good-bye.

"Hi, Karen!" said a girl dressed in a yellow jacket, blue jeans, and sneakers.

She looked like . . .

"Remember!" I cried.

"I am only called Remember when I am role-playing. My real name is Brianna Murphy. And this is my real mother," she said. "The special permission for me to come here today was from her!"

Brianna was not talking like a Pilgrim anymore. She was talking like a regular kid. Like me.

And her mother looked like a regular mother. She was wearing tan pants, brown loafers, and a red barn jacket. The suitcase behind her must have held the Pilgrim clothes.

"Hello, Karen," said Brianna's mother, smiling.

"This is so cool. You two are a real-life mother-daughter role-playing team," I said. "I wish my mom and I could be one too."

"Today we will be a real-life mother-daughter hospitality team," said Mommy. "Come, we will take our guests to the Rosebud Cafe."

"You will like it there," I said to Brianna. "They have sixty-one flavors of ice cream."

We piled into our car and drove to the ice-cream parlor. Brianna and I did not stop talking for a single minute.

At the Rosebud Cafe, we ordered ice-cream sundaes with everything on them. We each got three scoops of ice cream with syrup, whipped cream, sprinkles, nuts, and a cherry on top.

Brianna told me that she is in seventh grade. She lives with her mother, her father, three goldfish, two cats, and a dog.

It took me a long time to tell her about all the people and pets I live with!

She told me about her street and house in Massachusetts. They sounded a lot like my little-house street and house here in Stoney-brook. She even has two best friends.

We were laughing and talking so much, I forgot she had ever been a Pilgrim girl named Remember.

"Would you talk like a Pilgrim for me again?" I asked.

"All right," Brianna replied.

She closed her eyes for a minute. When

she opened them again, she was Remember.

"I am most grateful for this Thanksgiving feast," she said. "And I am truly happy to have met you, Karen Brewer."

I smiled. I was truly happy too.

19

Making Peace

It was the Wednesday before Thanksgiving. No special visitors were coming to school. But I could hardly wait to get to my classroom. I knew everyone would be talking about my presentation.

I was right. The kids asked me more questions about Plimoth Plantation. I felt like the official class Pilgrim.

The only one who did not seem so excited was Pamela. While the other kids crowded around me, she stayed at her desk with Jannie and Leslie. I saw her looking my way a few times.

She did not say one word to me at recess either. But I could see her sneaking peeks. My friends and I were playing games of Fox and Geese and talking like Pilgrim children.

"I can only play one more round," I said. "I promised Mother I would milk the goat before dinnertime."

"I must go grind corn. Mother and I are making hasty pudding," said Hannie.

"You two are lucky. It is my job to clean the pig's pen today," said Nancy.

"Eww!" we all said together.

(We knew real Pilgrims would not say that. But pretend Pilgrims could.)

When we returned to our classroom, Mr. Mackey, our art teacher, was waiting for us with his supply cart.

"Since tomorrow is Thanksgiving, we thought you might like to spend the afternoon making decorations to take home," said Ms. Colman.

Yippee! I felt as if the holiday had already started.

Mr. Mackey let us take the supplies we needed. But he did not stay, because he had other rooms to visit.

"Happy holiday, everyone," he said.

I was making a bouquet of paper flowers for Mommy and Seth. I had forgotten to get orange paper from Mr. Mackey. I knew some was in the supply closet, though. Pamela was already there. But I did not let that stop me.

I looked in the closet. Only one piece of orange paper was left. Pamela and I reached for it at the same time.

Since I was having such a good day already, I decided to be extra nice.

"You take it," I said. "I can use another color."

"No, that is okay. You go ahead," replied Pamela.

"I know what," I said. "We can cut it in half."

"Good idea," said Pamela.

I was glad we were trying to get along. I do not like fighting so much. Even with my best enemy.

While I was cutting the paper, Pamela said, "Your presentation was cool, Karen."

"Thank you," I replied. "Your presentation was cool too. And you have a really neat poppet doll."

"*You* have some really neat new friends," said Pamela.

I smiled. I would rather have real live friends than a doll any day.

I decided to make a few extra flowers to send Brianna.

20

Karen's Thanksgiving

"It is my turn!" said Andrew.

"Oh, all right," I replied.

I cranked the hand mixer three more times. Then I passed the bowl of cream to my little brother. The cream was just starting to turn to butter.

Mommy, Andrew, and I were making dinner. (Seth had said he needed to spend the morning working at his shop.) We were cooking delicious Pilgrim dishes. We were trying to cook them the Pilgrim way. Well, almost. Our oven was indoors. We did not have big pots over fires. And we did not have to go to a stream for our water.

Here is what we were making: cheate bread, butter, Indian corn pudding (we were using Remember's recipe), roast turkey with stuffing, butternut squash, and apple pie for dessert.

"Look, it really is butter!" said Andrew.

I looked into the bowl. The milky white cream was now thick and yellow. We had made our very own butter.

Mommy spread some on crackers for us to taste. "Next year we should not buy the cream. We should find a cow and milk her!" I said.

"You are a true Pilgrim girl," said Mommy.

We had fun cooking and tasting all morning.

It was almost noon when Seth came home. He was carrying three packages wrapped with colored ribbons. He gave one to Mommy, one to Andrew, and one to me.

"Go ahead and open them," he said.

"Wow! You made wooden bowls for us just like Remember's!" I said.

"These are beautiful," added Mommy. "Thank you."

We all thanked Seth. He had made a bowl for himself too. The bowls were going to make our Thanksgiving dinner even more like a Pilgrim feast.

That gave me an idea.

"When are we eating?" I asked.

"Soon," replied Mommy. "In fact, it is time for you to wash up and put on some holiday clothes."

Excellent! We were going to have an early dinner, just like the Pilgrims did. And holiday clothes were just what I had in mind.

I ran to my room and closed the door. It was not long before my closets and drawers were half empty. My bed and floor were covered with clothes. But I had everything I needed. Except for one thing. I could get it from Mommy later.

In a few minutes Mommy called, "Dinner is ready!" Mommy, Seth, and Andrew smiled as soon as they saw me coming down the stairs.

"Karen is a Pilgrim!" said Andrew.

"Welcome to our home, Pilgrim friend," said Seth. "Will you be our guest for Thanksgiving dinner?"

"I thank thee," I replied.

My clothes were not perfectly Pilgrim. But they were close enough. I had put on a long dark skirt. (I did not own any petticoats, so I had put a few skirts on to make me puffy.) I wore a button-up jacket.

"Here, Karen. You need this more than I do," said Mommy. She took off her white apron and tied it around my waist. That was the one last thing I needed.

We all carried food to the table. It smelled delicious. Before we ate, Seth had some Thanksgiving things to say.

"I am thankful for our health. I am thankful for this food. I am thankful for the free-

dom to enjoy this beautiful dinner with my family."

We held hands and sang a Thanksgiving song together. I sang it loud and clear.

Now that I knew the real story of the holiday, it was the happiest Thanksgiving ever.

L. GODWIN

About the Author

ANN M. MARTIN lives in New York City and loves animals, especially cats. She has two cats of her own, Gussie and Woody.

Other books by Ann M. Martin that you might enjoy are *Stage Fright*; *Me and Katie (the Pest)*; and the books in *The Baby-sitters Club* series.

Ann likes ice cream and *I Love Lucy*. And she has her own little sister, whose name is Jane.

Little Sister

Don't miss #92

KAREN'S SLEIGH RIDE

"Sleigh rides?" asked Elizabeth.

"Yes," I said. "During farm camp I saw an old sleigh way in the back of the Stones' little barn — the one that did not burn down. We can dust it off and use it. The Stones have a horse that can pull it. It has been snowing a whole, whole lot lately. So the horse can pull the sleigh over the snow. And we can charge money. And give the money to the Stones to rebuild their barn. Ta-daaa!"

BABY·SITTERS™

Little Sister

by Ann M. Martin
author of The Baby-sitters Club®

☐	MQ44300-3	#1	Karen's Witch	$2.95
☐	MQ44259-7	#2	Karen's Roller Skates	$2.95
☐	MQ44299-7	#3	Karen's Worst Day	$2.95
☐	MQ44264-3	#4	Karen's Kittycat Club	$2.95
☐	MQ44258-9	#5	Karen's School Picture	$2.95
☐	MQ44298-8	#6	Karen's Little Sister	$2.95
☐	MQ44257-0	#7	Karen's Birthday	$2.95
☐	MQ42670-2	#8	Karen's Haircut	$2.95
☐	MQ43652-X	#9	Karen's Sleepover	$2.95
☐	MQ43651-1	#10	Karen's Grandmothers	$2.95
☐	MQ43645-7	#15	Karen's In Love	$2.95
☐	MQ44823-4	#20	Karen's Carnival	$2.95
☐	MQ44824-2	#21	Karen's New Teacher	$2.95
☐	MQ44833-1	#22	Karen's Little Witch	$2.95
☐	MQ44832-3	#23	Karen's Doll	$2.95
☐	MQ44859-5	#24	Karen's School Trip	$2.95
☐	MQ44831-5	#25	Karen's Pen Pal	$2.95
☐	MQ44830-7	#26	Karen's Ducklings	$2.95
☐	MQ44829-3	#27	Karen's Big Joke	$2.95
☐	MQ44828-5	#28	Karen's Tea Party	$2.95
☐	MQ44825-0	#29	Karen's Cartwheel	$2.75
☐	MQ45645-8	#30	Karen's Kittens	$2.95
☐	MQ45646-6	#31	Karen's Bully	$2.95
☐	MQ45647-4	#32	Karen's Pumpkin Patch	$2.95
☐	MQ45648-2	#33	Karen's Secret	$2.95
☐	MQ45650-4	#34	Karen's Snow Day	$2.95
☐	MQ45652-0	#35	Karen's Doll Hospital	$2.95
☐	MQ45651-2	#36	Karen's New Friend	$2.95
☐	MQ45653-9	#37	Karen's Tuba	$2.95
☐	MQ45655-5	#38	Karen's Big Lie	$2.95
☐	MQ45654-7	#39	Karen's Wedding	$2.95
☐	MQ47040-X	#40	Karen's Newspaper	$2.95
☐	MQ47041-8	#41	Karen's School	$2.95
☐	MQ47042-6	#42	Karen's Pizza Party	$2.95
☐	MQ46912-6	#43	Karen's Toothache	$2.95
☐	MQ47043-4	#44	Karen's Big Weekend	$2.95
☐	MQ47044-2	#45	Karen's Twin	$2.95
☐	MQ47045-0	#46	Karen's Baby-sitter	$2.95
☐	MQ46913-4	#47	Karen's Kite	$2.95
☐	MQ47046-9	#48	Karen's Two Families	$2.95
☐	MQ47047-7	#49	Karen's Stepmother	$2.95
☐	MQ47048-5	#50	Karen's Lucky Penny	$2.95
☐	MQ48229-7	#51	Karen's Big Top	$2.95
☐	MQ48299-8	#52	Karen's Mermaid	$2.95
☐	MQ48300-5	#53	Karen's School Bus	$2.95
☐	MQ46301-3	#54	Karen's Candy	$2.95
☐	MQ48230-0	#55	Karen's Magician	$2.95
☐	MQ48302-1	#56	Karen's Ice Skates	$2.95
☐	MQ48303-X	#57	Karen's School Mystery	$2.95
☐	MQ48304-8	#58	Karen's Ski Trip	$2.95

More Titles... ➡

The Baby-sitters Little Sister titles continued...

Available wherever you buy books, or use this order form.

Scholastic Inc., P.O. Box 7502, Jefferson City, MO 65102

Please send me the books I have checked above. I am enclosing $_____
(please add $2.00 to cover shipping and handling). Send check or money order – no
cash or C.O.Ds please.

Name_____Birthdate_____

Address_____

City_____State/Zip_____

LITTLE 🍎 APPLE®

Here are some of our favorite Little Apples.

There are fun times ahead with kids just like you in Little Apple books! Once you take a bite out of a Little Apple—you'll want to read more!

Reading Excitement for Kids with BIG Appetites!

☐ NA45899-X **Amber Brown Is Not a Crayon**
  Paula Danziger $2.99

☐ NA93425-2 **Amber Brown Goes Fourth**
  Paula Danziger $2.99

☐ NA50207-7 **You Can't Eat Your Chicken Pox, Amber Brown**
  Paula Danziger $2.99

☐ NA42833-0 **Catwings** Ursula K. LeGuin $2.95

☐ NA42832-2 **Catwings Return** Ursula K. LeGuin $3.50

☐ NA41-821-1 **Class Clown** Johanna Hurwitz $2.99

☐ NA42400-9 **Five True Horse Stories**
  Margaret Davidson $2.99

☐ NA43868-9 **The Haunting of Grade Three**
  Grace Maccarone $2.99

☐ NA40966-2 **Rent a Third Grader** B.B. Hiller $2.99

☐ NA41944-7 **The Return of the Third Grade Ghost Hunters**
  Grace Maccarone $2.99

☐ NA42031-3 **Teacher's Pet** Johanna Hurwitz $3.50

Available wherever you buy books...or use the coupon below.

- -

SCHOLASTIC INC., P.O. Box 7502, 2931 East McCarty Street, Jefferson City, MO 65102

Please send me the books I have checked above. I am enclosing $ _____ (please add $2.00 to cover shipping and handling). Send check or money order—no cash or C.O.D.s please.

Name_____

Address_____

City_____ **State/Zip**_____

Please allow four to six weeks for delivery. Offer good in the U.S.A. only. Sorry, mail orders are not available to residents of Canada. Prices subject to change.   LA996